P9-DBM-392

Dear Parent:

Congratulations! Your child is taking the first steps on an exciting journey. The destination? Independent reading!

STEP INTO READING® will help your child get there. The program offers five steps to reading success. Each step includes fun stories and colorful art. There are also Step into Reading Sticker Books, Step into Reading Math Readers, Step into Reading Phonics Readers, Step into Reading Write-In Readers, and Step into Reading Phonics Boxed Sets—a complete literacy program with something for every child.

Learning to Read, Step by Step!

Ready to Read   Preschool–Kindergarten
• big type and easy words • rhyme and rhythm • picture clues
For children who know the alphabet and are eager to begin reading.

Reading with Help   Preschool–Grade 1
• basic vocabulary • short sentences • simple stories
For children who recognize familiar words and sound out new words with help.

Reading on Your Own   Grades 1–3
• engaging characters • easy-to-follow plots • popular topics
For children who are ready to read on their own.

Reading Paragraphs   Grades 2–3
• challenging vocabulary • short paragraphs • exciting stories
For newly independent readers who read simple sentences with confidence.

Ready for Chapters   Grades 2–4
• chapters • longer paragraphs • full-color art
For children who want to take the plunge into chapter books but still like colorful pictures.

STEP INTO READING® is designed to give every child a successful reading experience. The grade levels are only guides. Children can progress through the steps at their own speed, developing confidence in their reading, no matter what their grade.

Remember, a lifetime love of reading starts with a single step!

BARBIE and associated trademarks and trade dress are owned by, and used under license from, Mattel.
Copyright © 2018 Mattel. All Rights Reserved.
www.barbie.com
Published in the United States by Random House Children's Books, a division of Penguin Random House LLC, 1745 Broadway, New York, NY 10019, and in Canada by Penguin Random House Canada Limited, Toronto.

Step into Reading, Random House, and the Random House colophon are registered trademarks of Penguin Random House LLC.

Visit us on the Web!
StepIntoReading.com
rhcbooks.com

Educators and librarians, for a variety of teaching tools, visit us at RHTeachersLibrarians.com

ISBN 978-1-5247-6883-6 (trade) — ISBN 978-1-5247-6891-1 (lib. bdg.)

Printed in the United States of America   10 9 8 7 6 5 4 3 2 1

Random House Children's Books supports the First Amendment and celebrates the right to read.

Barbie™
Let's Plant a Garden!

by Kristen L. Depken
illustrated by Dynamo Limited

Random House 🏠 New York

It is springtime!

Barbie and her sisters
want to plant a garden.

They pick a spot.

They spread fresh dirt.

They dig.

The girls use shovels.

The puppies use
their paws!

Barbie plants roses.

Skipper plants tomatoes.

Stacie plants berries.

Chelsea plants daisies.

Uh-oh!

There is no more space!

Barbie has an idea.

They will plant
a garden
for the town!

They spread fresh dirt.

People from town help.

They plant fruit.

They plant vegetables.

They plant flowers.
They water the garden.

Soon,

everything blooms!

Everyone takes home fruit, vegetables, and flowers.

What a lovely garden!

3252